LONE WOLF and CUB

by

KAZUO KOIKE

and

GOSEKI KOJIMA

cover by

FRANK MILLER

and

LYNN VARLEY

第12巻

剛 一
夕 夫

FIRST PUBLISHING

Kazuo Koike
STORY

Goseki Kojima
ART

Frank Miller
COVER ILLUSTRATION & INTRODUCTION

David Lewis, Alex Wald
ENGLISH ADAPTATION

Willie Schubert
LETTERING

Paul Guinan
PRODUCTION

Rick Oliver
EDITOR

Rick Obadiah
PUBLISHER

Alex Wald
ART DIRECTOR

Kathy Kotsivas
OPERATIONS DIRECTOR

Mike McCormick
PRODUCTION MANAGER

Kurt Goldzung
SALES DIRECTOR

For him, the battle never ends. Every shadow on every shadowed roadside must be studied, and felt for the smell and sound of hidden enemies. On the road, in the dusty grey villages, there are only stangers, and the strangers' faces, the fearful merchant, the smiling geisha, the bleary-eyed drunk, the faces are all masks, a sad parade of masks, and he must look deep into the eyes of each of them, and be ready for the flash of hateful recognition, the sudden silent streak of sharpened steel.

For him, for his boy, there is no hope. Only the blades and the ninja, charging and falling in waves, their blood a river, a frothing ocean. Only the lost ones, wailing and dying in a world gone mad.

Was there a time when he was honored by his people? Was there a woman, warm and loving in his arms, her belly swollen with his son? Is there behind him, past the mountains, a beginning to this desolate pathway?

Yes . . . but now there is only the shallow breathing of his sleeping boy, the pebbles beneath his naked feet, the low rumble of the wooden cart, the windless night.

Frank Miller
Los Angeles 1988

序文

EXECUTIONER'S HILL

其之十三

首丘
（しゆ きゆう）

君子曰く

礼記

皐はその自ら生ずる所を楽しむ

礼はその本を忘れず

古の人に言あり

曰く狼死て正しく丘に首するは

たなり

楚辞

鳥は飛んで故郷に反り

狼は死するに必ず丘に首す

It is writ in the REIXI:

The true man of virtue rejoices in that which he
he has made and forgets not the models of
rectitude. For thus was it said of old, that the
dying wolf turns his head respectfully to the
hills. Thus is virtue.

It is writ in the SOJI:

The birds bend their wings toward home.
The wolf turns his head to the hills to die.

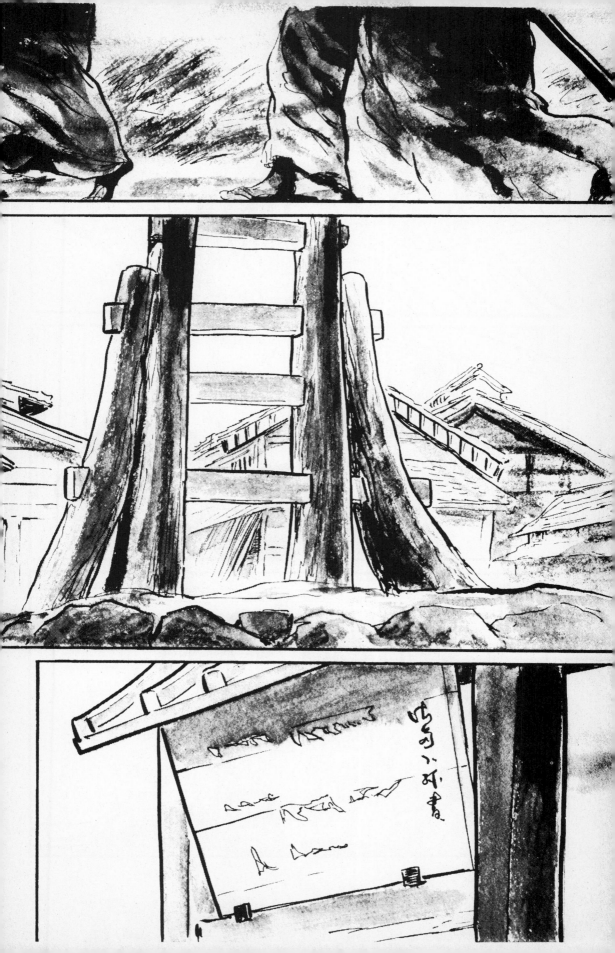

HEY! DON'T YOU GOT NO GOVERNMENT OFFICIAL?

N-NO SIR. THERE'S JUST ME.

DAMN. JUST ONE LOUSY WATCH-DOG.

ARE THERE NO NEW BOUNTY LISTS?

NO, SIR. THESE DAYS THERE IS NOTHING AT ALL, SIR.

WHERE'S THE SAKE?!

W-WHO ON EARTH ARE Y-YOU GENTLE-MEN?

COME OFF IT! DON'T YOU *RECOGNIZE* US? WE'RE THE *HIGH NOON* GANG!

THE *BOUNTY HUNTERS?!*

I'D *DIDN'T* REALIZE!

NOW, HOW ABOUT THAT *SAKE?!*

I-I'VE GOT A *LITTLE* FOR WHEN I GO TO BED.

DISH IT OUT! THE HIGH NOON GANG TAKES CARE OF YOUR HEAD-ACHES, DON'T IT? WE *CLEAN OUT* YOUR CRIMINALS FOR YOU, SWEEP UP YOUR TRASH. WE'RE YOUR *JANITORS!* YOU OUGHTA BE BUST-ING YOUR BUTT TO DO *RIGHT* BY US!

Y-YES, SIR.

GLUCK
GLUCK
GLUCK

WELL NOW, WATCHDOG-- DON'T YOU GOT NO *WORK* FOR US? MURDERS, BODYGUARDS, YOU NAME IT. *ANYTHING GOES.*

WORK? FOR THE LIKES OF YOU GENTLEMEN? WE DON'T HAVE ANYTHING.

DAMN! NOWADAYS WE'RE PRACTICALLY *UNEMPLOYED!* THE *BOTTOM* OF THE *BARREL!*

WHAT SHOULD WE DO, *SHIWASU?**

WE HAVE NO *CHOICE.* WE GO SOMEWHERE WHERE WE CAN FIND WORK.

SHIWASU-- YAKUZA (GANGSTER) DIALECT FOR BOSS.

CAN'T DO NOTHING IF THERE'S NO ONE FOR US TO *KILL*. USED TO BE *TWELVE* OF US AND NOW WE'RE DOWN TO *SIX*. HIGH NOON GANG NOTHING, WE'RE A HALF-ASSED "SUNSET" GANG.

THE WORLD'S GOTTEN *PEACEFUL* TOO DAMN *FAST!*

13

KEIMA! *TAIL HIM!*

HUH?

WE'VE *FOUND* WORK, *BIG* WORK! TAIL THAT *RONIN* * AND TRACK DOWN HIS *LAIR.*

YES, SIR!

RONIN--A MASTERLESS SAMURAI.   16

THIS IS IT, BOYS. A REALLY BIG JOB!

YOU THINK WE CAN GET *WORK* OUT OF THAT RONIN AND HIS *BRAT?*

WHAT D'YOU MEAN SHIWASU?

HE'S *ITTO OGAMI,* THE SHOGUN'S *OFFICER OF DEATH!*

WHAT?!

THAT RONIN WAS LONE WOLF?

YOU'RE SURE?

LONE WOLF AND CUB!

I HEARD THAT OGAMI FEUDED WITH THE *YAGYU* CLAN AND WAS *BANISHED* FROM HIS POST.* HE WAS RUMORED TO BE TRAVELLING THE COUNTRYSIDE AS AN *ASSASSIN*, LONE WOLF AND CUB. I *SCARCELY* BELIEVED IT.

THERE'S NO MISTAKE. THAT FACE. AND CARRYING *DOTANUKI*, HIS BATTLE SWORD! HOW CAN I EVER FORGET? HE *KILLED* MY YOUNG LORD** AND *DESTROYED* OUR CLAN! EVER SINCE THEN I'VE WANDERED *MASTERLESS* LIKE A RABID WOLF. SCRATCHING FOR A LIVING LIKE A MISERABLE BOUNTY HUNTER!

HOW CAN I FORGET? HOW HARD I TRIED TO FORGET.

SO...TWO WOLVES QUARREL. WHAT'S IN IT FOR *US*?

*LONE WOLF AND CUB #1 AND #6.

20

**LONE WOLF AND CUB #6.

I'VE HEARD RUMORS THAT HE GETS 500 RYO IN GOLD FOR EACH HEAD.

TEN ASSASSINATIONS, 5,000 RYO! TWENTY ASSASSINATIONS, 10,000 RYO!

DON'T TELL ME HE CARRIES ALL THAT *WITH* HIM.

BUT IF HE'S GOT THAT MUCH *GOLD*, WHAT'S HE ROAMING THE COUNTRYSIDE FOR? THE TWO OF THEM CAN SPEND THEIR LIVES IN *LUXURY!*

IT'S LIKE JINZA SAYS. IF HE HAS THAT MUCH MONEY, HE WOULDN'T BE WALKING AROUND LIKE A *BEGGAR* IN RAGS.

IT WOULD TAKE MORE THAN 10,000 RYO TO DESTROY THE *YAGYU* CLAN.

WHAT?!

I FIGURE HE'D NEED AT LEAST 50,000 RYO TO SHOWER ON *SHOGUNATE* OFFICIALS.

AND HE'D STILL NEED TO *REBUILD* THE OGAMI CLAN, EVEN WHILE FIGHTING THE YAGYU THEMSELVES.

AND IF IT COST HIM HIS LIFE, HIS SON WOULD CARRY THE FIGHT.

HMMM. GIVING GOLD TO THE SHOGUNATE TO RIGHT THE YAGYU'S WRONGS...

NOT IMPOSSIBLE.

IF OUR HAN HAD 50,000 RYO, WE MIGHT HAVE BEEN ABLE TO *BUY OFF* THE ELDERS. WE MIGHT HAVE *SAVED* THE CLAN FROM *DISSOLUTION.*

I GUESS.

IN THIS WORLD YOU CAN BUY ANYONE BUT THE SHOGUN HIMSELF.

YOU THINK THAT'S WHY HE'S ROVING ABOUT LIKE A WILD WOLF, *HOARDING* THE MONEY HE GETS FOR MURDER?

IF HE BECAME AN *ASSASSIN* NOT TO LIVE, BUT TO *DESTROY* THE YAGYU...

THEN THERE'S *MONEY!*

ALL RIGHT!

LET'S DO IT!

23

HIS *SUIO* SCHOOL HORSE-SLASHING STROKE DEFEATED THE *YAGYU* GUARDS!

REMEMBER, THIS MAN USED TO BE *KOGI KAISHAKUNIN,* THE OFFICER OF DEATH.

WHAT OF YOUR OWN *MUGAI* SCHOOL MAN-KILLING SWORD, SHIWASU? CAN'T YOU *BEAT* HIM?

NOT EVEN WITH YOUR *GEKKEN* SCHOOL SPORT-SPEAR, JINZA SHIMOTSUKI.

IN THAT CASE, ALL *FIVE* OF US WILL TAKE HIM TO-GETHER.

WE'RE NOT OUT TO FENCE WITH HIM.

THE FIRST THING IS TO MAKE HIM *TELL* US WHERE HE KEEPS THE GOLD!

HOW ABOUT *NABBING* THE *BRAT?*

KIDNAPPING A *CHILD?* I DON'T MUCH LIKE IT.

THAT'S THE *BEST* WAY. IF HE REALLY PLANS TO *DESTROY* THE *YAGYU* AND *REBUILD* HIS HOUSEHOLD, THEN OBVIOUSLY HE'LL LEAVE EVERYTHING TO HIS *BOY.* IF HE LOSES HIS SON, HE LOSES *ALL.*

FORGET THAT, *JINZA.* FORGET YOU WERE EVER A *SAMURAI.*

WE DON'T WANT A FIGHT.

GOLD!

THE *WOLF'S GOLD.*

THAT'S ALL WE WANT!

RATTLE RATTLE RATTLE

HE'S LAID UP IN A *HUT* BY THE RIVER.

MUST HAVE FIGURED HE COULDN'T GET ANYWHERE IN THIS *SANDSTORM.*

GOOD.

GINJI.

YES, SIR!

PAT PAT

HOW WOULD *YOU* NAB THE BOY?

KRANK PLOO!

HEY, LEAVE THAT TO ME!

THE *BEST* WAY TO HOOK A KID IS BY THE *EAR.* HA HA HA. JUST WAIT AND SEE.

teketeke teketeke ten ten ten

teketeke
teketeke
ten
ten
ten

WHEN YOU'RE FLUSHING *GAME*, YOU USE THE *OIZEKO* DRUM.

TO CATCH A *KID*, PLAY THE *CANDY SELLER* SONG.

THE *47 RONIN* * PLAYED THE BATTLE-FIELD DRUM! PULL IN THE RUBES WITH THE *HIGH TOWER* DRUM. THE *KAMURO* DRUM'S FOR THE *LIBERTINES.*

*47 RONIN -- SAMURAI WHO COMMITTED RITUAL SUICIDE AFTER FAILING IN THEIR ATTEMPT TO AVENGE THE DEATH OF THEIR MASTER AT THE HANDS OF THE SHOGUN.

NOW!

NO!

THUMP THUMP THUMP

GET THE KID WHILE YOU CAN!

I'LL TAKE THE PAPA WOLF!

THAP THAP THAP

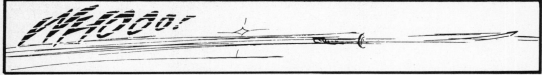

RRR!

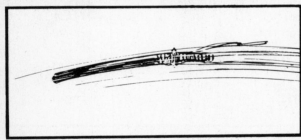

FANCY MEETING YOU HERE, LORD OGAMI.

HEH HEH HEH

38

NO DOUBT YOU DON'T *REMEMBER* ME. BUT I REMEMBER YOU. VERY VERY WELL.

AFTER ALL, I SAW YOU *EXECUTE* MY YOUNG LORD! HE PLACED HIS *FAN* TO HIS STOMACH, YOU SWUNG YOUR SWORD, HIS *HEAD* FELL. HAHAHA!

IF WE CUT *YOUR BOY'S* HEAD, WE MERELY FOLLOW THE WILL OF OUR YOUNG LORD. *REVENGE!*

BUT IN THIS WORLD OF *POVERTY* AND WOE, REVENGE WON'T *BUY* YOU A SQUARE MEAL.

TELL US WHERE YOU'VE *STASHED* THE GOLD YOU'VE GOTTEN FOR YOUR ASSASSINATIONS. WE'LL LET BYGONES BE BYGONES.

HOW ABOUT IT?!

39

IF YOU LOSE THE BOY, ALL YOUR HOPES FOR THE FUTURE ARE OVER.

SPIT IT OUT! WHERE'S THE GOLD!?

YOU CAN ALWAYS EARN MORE MONEY!

THIS BATTLE'S LOST!

WHAT SAY YOU, ITTO OGAMI!?!

NEVER!

WHAT?! YOU DON'T *CARE* IF I *SLICE* HIS HEAD OFF?!

IF YOU THINK YOU *CAN,* CUT IT OFF!

THERE'S *NOTHING* IN IT FOR YOU IF YOU DO.

W*HAT*?!

YOU THINK WE'RE *BLUFFING?*

NOT AT ALL. BUT IF THE BOY *DIES,* I WILL KILL YOU ALL.

BODIES AND DUST WILL BE ALL THAT REMAIN.

B-BUT, ANY FATHER WISHES TO *SAVE* HIS CHILD! YOU, MOST OF ALL! HE'S THE *KEY* TO *ACHIEVING* YOUR GOAL...

YOUR AIM IS *MONEY.* KILLING THE CHILD WON'T BRING YOU *GOLD.*

FATHER AND SON, WE LIVE BY *MEIFU MADO!* THE *DARK ROAD* TO *HELL!*

IF I LOSE *EVERYTHING,* HERE AND NOW, THAT IS THE *FATE* THAT HELL HAS LED ME TO. IT IS *BEYOND* MY *POWER!*

THEN LET ME ASK...

YOU *SAW* US-- YOU SAW YOUR SON WAS IN *DANGER.* WHY DID YOU RUSH TO HIS *AID?*

WHAT OTHER REASON THAN A FATHER'S LOVE?!

WE *BATTLE* DANGER, WE *STRIVE* TO THE LAST. THEN, WHEN WE HAVE EXHAUSTED OUR POWERS, WE *AWAIT* OUR FATE. WHAT COULD BE MORE *NATURAL?* IS THERE ANYONE WHO SURRENDERS FROM THE BEGINNING?

D-DAMN IT! I *MEAN* IT!

I *REALLY* WILL KILL HIM!

MAKE NO *MISTAKE.* OUR OBJECT IS MONEY. WE GAIN NOTHING FROM KILLING THE BOY.

SO, YOU ACCEPT MEIFU MADO?

YOU BRING UP FORGOTTEN *MEMORIES!* I, TOO, ONCE BURNED WITH RAGE AGAINST THE SHOGUNATE.

I *SWORE* TO LIVE BY MEIFU MADO. I *SWORE* I WOULD CHARGE INTO THE SHOGUN'S PROCESSION, BY MYSELF IF I HAD TO, TO KILL MY *DAIMYO'S* * ENEMY.

43

*DAIMYO--A FEUDAL LORD.

PHEW!

ONE YEAR PASSED. TWO YEARS PASSED. BEFORE LONG I WAS THINKING ONLY OF HOW TO LIVE ANOTHER DAY, WHERE TO FIND *FOOD*, WHERE TO *SLEEP*...

IN THE END, DAMNED IF I COULDN'T EVEN REMEMBER MY LORD'S FACE!

W-WHAT'S G-GOT INTO YOU GUYS! *FINISH* HIM OFF QUICK!

DON'T LET HIM *DOUBLE-TALK* YOU. HE'S TWISTING WORDS TO GET THE ADVANTAGE! HIS TONGUE'S A *SWORD!*

SHUT UP!

DO YOU KNOW WHAT IT MEANS TO LIVE BY MEIFU MADO? IT MEANS LEAVING IT TO THE BOY TO *CHOOSE* LIFE OR DEATH!

IF HE CHOOSES *DEATH*, HIS FATHER WILL KILL HIM BY HIS *OWN HAND!*

THIS KIND OF LIFE IS MORE *PAINFUL* THAN DYING! HOW MUCH *EASIER* IS DEATH!

YOU'RE A *YAKUZA!* A GANGSTER AND AN *OUTCAST!* YOU MUST HAVE FELT THIS ONCE IN YOUR LIFE!

AN ASSASSIN WITH CHILD.

HE MUST BE BOTH SHACKLES AND CHAINS, A *BURDEN* ON YOUR WORK. BUT IF YOU LIVE BY MEIFU MADO, THEN YOUR WAY OF THE ASSASSIN MAKES *SENSE*, EVEN WITH A CHILD.

BUT THERE'S NO PULLING BACK NOW.

RELEASE THE CHILD!

B-BUT--

45

WE MIS-CALCULATED. WE WON'T ASK WHERE YOU HIDE THE GOLD.

BUT--!

IF WE TAKE *YOUR* HEAD TO THE AUTHORITIES, THAT WILL BE *WORTH* SOMETHING!

THE YAGYU WOULD *PAY* REAL MONEY FOR THAT!

YEAH. IT NEVER OCCURED TO ME. ITTO OGAMI'S *HEAD* WOULD BRING PLENTY OF GOLD.

HA HA HA! NOW WE'RE THINKING LIKE BOUNTY HUNTERS!

JINZA SHIMOTSUKI, GEKKAN SCHOOL!

IKKAKU SHIWASU, MUGAI SCHOOL!

WE'LL HAVE THAT HEAD!

GINJI OF KEIMA!

THE SUIO SCHOOL.

ITTO OGAMI!

CAW

CAW

SUUU!

KYAH!!

HYA!!

53

KYIAH!

GARGH!

SHUNK!

URRNGH!

AAUGH!

WAAA!

SHUUU!

PAPA!

THE BIRDS BENT THEIR WINGS TOWARD HOME.
THE WOLF TURNS HIS HEAD TO THE HILLS TO DIE.

BUT AROUND THIS FATED FATHER AND CHILD
THE WILD DOGS GATHER, SEEKING TO REND
THEIR WINGS AND TEAR EVEN THEIR BODIES
IN DEATH.

KAZUO KOIKE

Kazuo Koike is considered to be one of Japan's most successful writers and a master scriptwriter for the graphic story genre. He is perhaps best known in the U.S. for his screenplay for the feature film "Shogun Assassin," a re-edited version of the Japanese film "Kozure Okami," based on the **Lone Wolf and Cub** stories. Mr. Koike currently operates a publishing/production company for comics, Studio Ship, Inc., which publishes the works of Japan's major comics writers and artists in both book and magazine format. Mr. Koike is also the founder of Gekiga-Sonjuko, a school which offers a two year course for aspiring professional artists and writers.

GOSEKI KOJIMA

Goseki Kojima made his debut as a comic artist in 1967 with "Oboro-Junin-Cho." With his unique style Mr. Kojima created a new form of expressive visual interpretation for the graphic storytelling medium, and established for himself a position as a master craftsman with his ground-breaking work on **Lone Wolf and Cub**. Other works by Mr. Kojima in collaboration with Mr. Koike are "Kawaite Soro," "Kubikiri Asa," "Hanzo-No-Mon," "Tatamidori Kasajiro," "Do-Chi-Shi," and "Bohachi Bushido."

小池一夫　小島剛夕

The prequel to the saga of *Lone Wolf and Cub* reveals the events that led to Itto Ogami's appointment as the Shogun's officer of death — and the origins of the dreaded Yagyu's plot to overthrow Ogami and seize control of the Shogunate.

来月